Wanda

By Sihle Nontshokweni and Mathabo Tlali
Illustrated by Chantelle and Burgen Thorne

Crocodile Books, USA
An imprint of Interlink Publishing Group, Inc.
www.interlinkbooks.com

To friendships that provoke learning, unlearning, and thinking beyond self.
To young Black women, who learned that their hair was a burden and not a crown,
we hope this story will lead you to return to the places in your heart where you
continue to hide, only to feel unseen.

We hope that you find and feel
the memories and hurt so that you
may heal and be free.

First American edition published in 2021 by
Crocodile Books
An imprint of Interlink Publishing Group, Inc.
46 Crosby Street, Northampton, MA 01060
www.interlinkbooks.com

Text copyright © Sihle Nontshokweni and Mathabo Tlali, 2019
Illustrations copyright © Chantelle and Burgen Thorne, 2019

Original published in South Africa by
Jacana Media (Pty) Ltd in 2019

Library of Congress Cataloging-in-Publication Data
Names: Nontshokweni, Sihle, author. |
    Tlali, Mathabo, author. | Thorne,
    Chantelle, illustrator. | Thorne, Burgen, illustrator.
Title: Wanda / by Sihle Nontshokweni and Mathabo
    Tlali ; illustrated by Chantelle and Burgen Thorne.
Description: First American edition. |
    Northampton, MA : Crocodile Books,
    2020. | Original published in South Africa
    by Jacana Media (Pty) Ltd in 2019. |
    Audience: Ages 3-8. | Audience: Grades K-1. |
    Summary: Eight-year-old Wanda is unhappy due
    to the endless mocking of her hair by the boys at
    school, but when Makhulu (grandmother) shares her
    grooming secrets and stories of beautiful women with
    locks just like Wanda, she realizes her hair is a crown
    and is something to be proud of.
Identifiers: LCCN 2020039137 | ISBN 9781623718640 (hardback)
Subjects: CYAC: Hair--Fiction. | Self-confidence--Fiction. | Blacks--South
    Africa--Fiction. | South Africa--Fiction.
Classification: LCC PZ7.1.N6395 Wan 2020 | DDC [E]--dc23
LC record available at https://lccn.loc.gov/2020039137

Printed and bound in Korea

Wanda

By Sihle Nontshokweni and Mathabo Tlali

Illustrated by Chantelle and Burgen Thorne

Wanda races to the bus stop.

She trips and falls.

When she looks up she sees the school bus.

"Oh no!

Stop the bus!"

Wanda waves and gallops like
a horse to get to the bus.

Tat' uBhejula, their bus driver, is not pleased.

"You're late!"

Wanda sits down. "I made it," she says.
Then she hears Thula and Sizwe's voices.

"*Hey you!* You are always huffing and puffing, shouting, 'Stop the bus!'" they say, making fun of her.
"Miss Bush! Miss Bush!"
they shout, pointing at her hair.

She frowns and repeats the words her mother says to her every morning: "I am a queen and this is my crown," she says, pointing to her head.

"A queen with a crown?" Sizwe says, giggling. "I forget you have a wonderful imagination."

Wanda lifts her head proudly, just like the many beautiful women on Mlungiseleli Drive.

She hears Mama's words:

"*Intombi mayizithembe*, Wanda. A young girl must always remain confident."

So she puts on a brave face, but she is haunted by the ticking of the clock.

"Tat' uBhejula must drive faster," she thinks. She has to get to school early enough for her "big switch."

No one knows that Wanda changes the "cloud" that her mother combs so beautifully.

She changes it to something that her teacher, Mrs. Stone, calls "neat and clean for a Lady in Green."

"No one else seems to struggle like me," she thinks.
"My hair is a crown, but one made of thorns."

The next day, the bus is late.

Thula and Sizwe, like two proud hyenas, tease her,
but she does not look at them.
Their cackles are whooshed away by her thoughts.
She imagines that her hair is smooth like a superhero's cape.

The bus reaches the school gate just as the bell rings.
Wanda is frantic!

Tears stream down her face.
She doesn't have time to make the big switch.
She runs to join her class line.

"I will get a black dot on my star chart.
She will say it's a bird's nest.
She's said this to other girls before!"

Wanda holds her breath.
Mrs. Stone starts to walk down the line.

Wanda can no longer feel herself breathe.

The whole class turns to watch.

She wishes the earth would open up and hide her away.

She tries to hide behind the boy in front of her.

Mrs. Stone seems to tower over her.

"The bus was late for school ... I could not fix my hair.

I'm sorry, ma'am."

But in her head the words are different.

"My mother says my hair is strong
and beautiful like clouds.
I say so too. I love my hair
and one day I will be
brave enough to say so."

Noticing Wanda's frightened eyes, Mrs. Stone takes pity on her.
"Find a headband in the lost property box," she says sternly.

Wanda finds a headband. She imagines Thula and Sizwe
laughing at her. She tries to be brave.

"Be confident," she reminds herself.
She tries to find her own sway and go about her school day.

After school she walks home. A heavy walk. No sway.
"Maybe Thula and Sizwe are right; maybe I am not a queen,"
she says to herself as she chokes on her tears.

At the front gate she tries to make the last big switch of the day.
Her ten tiny fingers run through her flattened hair, trying to puff it out.

Wanda walks into the kitchen to the brightest smile and wide-open arms. Arms ready to swallow all the sadness in her eight-year-old body.

"*Makhulu*," Wanda says. She buries herself in Makhulu's arms.

"*Kumkanikazi*," her grandmother says warmly.

"I am not a queen, Makhulu," Wanda wails.
"I don't want this hair."

"You are a queen and your hair
IS your crown," Makhulu says gently.

"Your mom told me that you were having problems with your hair and I came with gifts fit for a queen."

Makhulu takes out a scrapbook. To Wanda's surprise, the first page is filled with pictures of beautiful women wearing hairstyles she has never seen before.

"Woooow, Makhulu," she says in wonder.

"Her hair is tall like Tat' uVuka's peach tree," Wanda says. "This lady's hair is so curly and pretty it looks like the rose bush in Makhulu Violet's house."

Makhulu cannot hide her smile as Wanda talks about the hairstyles on the page.

"Makhulu, who are these women?"

"Aaah," Makhulu says with pride. "This is Diana Ross.
This one is Winnie Madikizela-Mandela. This is Brenda Fassie...

Shado Twala ... Angelique Kidjo ... and this one is my favorite,
Miriam Makeba, the Rihanna of my time."
They both laugh.

Makhulu turns to the last page. "That's Mama!" Wanda says.

Makhulu chuckles. "Yes, it is. And that is me," she says, pointing to the second picture. Wanda gasps because her mother was right. Makhulu's hair, just like her mother's hair, and just like her own hair, is beautiful.

Makhulu pulls a picture out of her bag.

Wanda looks at it and a smile fills her face.

"Look, I was a tiny baby with big hair."

"Yes, you were," Makhulu says.

"Perfect,"
they both laugh.

"Every crown has its secret,"
Makhulu says to Wanda.
"Bring me my special comb."

Wanda expects each rake of the comb to be painful.
But instead Makhulu sprays a magical mist, which
softens Wanda's coarse hair.

"Which hairstyle do you want?"
Wanda chooses from the scrapbook.

"Makhulu, what is the secret to my crown?" Wanda asks.

"Water and
100% olive oil,"
Makhulu responds.

The next day, Wanda calmly greets Tat' uBhejula.

There are no hyena voices buzzing in her ears.

The boys are quiet as they watch Wanda take her seat.

Thula sits with his mouth wide open. Sizwe is shocked.

"You look like a queen," Thula says.

And, like the beautiful and proud
women from Mlungiseleli Drive,
Wanda looks straight ahead.
She pays no attention to silly boys.

This time, she truly knows
she looks like a queen.

Kumkanikazi – a queen

Makhulu – grandmother

Intombi mayizithembe –
A young girl must always remain
confident. This is an African proverb
that girls are raised on to lift their
confidence and their ability to
navigate young adulthood. It is
often said as a reminder to carry
oneself with pride, and it carries
multiple connotations including
how one interacts with boys.